'Keeping Fit with Caz and

Keep your bodies
MOVING!

Stories by Melissa Lavi ©   Published in Hong Kong by Melissa Lavi

And a one
and a two,
and it's 'tennis'
time with you.

And a three
and a four,
and a serve
right from your core.

What an 'ACE'!
What a shot!
That ball really
hit the spot.

Here it comes.
Watch him fret.
No! it's gone
in to the net.

I have to
focus more,
now we're at
an even score.

We've made
it to a 'deuce'.
Let's take five,
and have some juice.

No! another
point for him.
Looks like
he's going to win.

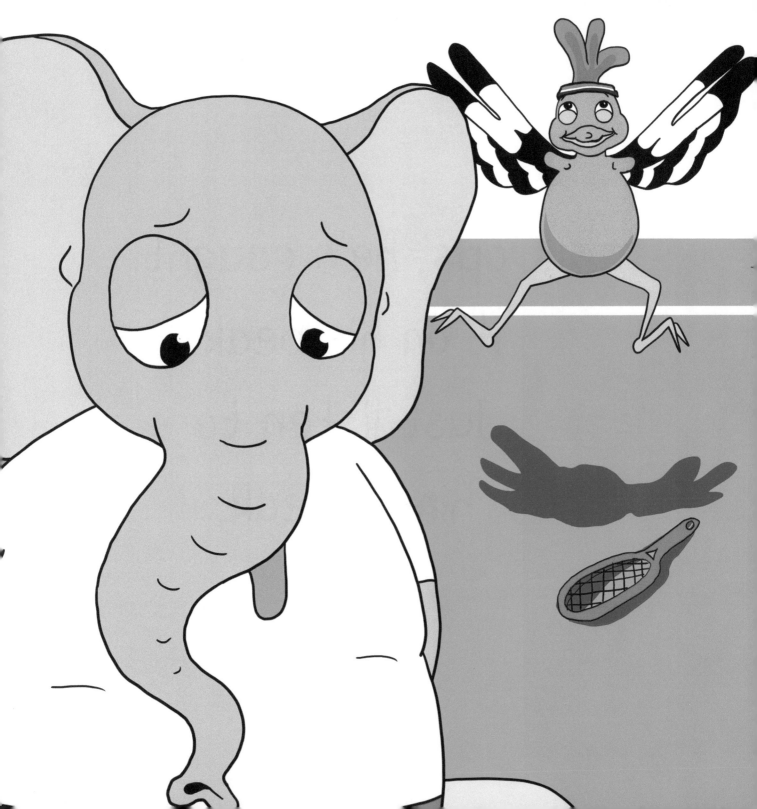

Oops, he's caught
it on his beak.
Just listen to
him squeak.

I am going to
make my move,
with a slam,
bam, hit and groove.

Match point is
edging in,
and I really
want to win.

I just need a
a winning bash,
and my strongest
ever smash!

Oops, it's gone
little high.
Looks like a rocket
in the sky!

But that perfect
landing patch,
makes it
'GAME'
'SET'
and
'MATCH'

And the only way to

STOP!

is with a

FABULICIOUS

DROP

DA-DAAA

Caz and Kit
love
Keeping
fit.

Be sure to try it too!

CPSIA information can be obtained
at www.ICGtesting.com
Printed in the USA
LVHW071948141019
634123LV00002B/302/P